MR. BUMP

by Roger Hargreaves

This is the sad story of Mr Bump.

The trouble was that Mr Bump just could not help having little accidents.

If there was something for Mr Bump to bump into, he'd bump into it all right.

For instance.

If you were to see Mr Bump out walking down a street in your town, and if there happened to be something to bump into down that street, then you know what would happen, don't you?

BUMP!

Mr Bump was just the same at home.

He lived in an extremely nice home, but even there he couldn't help having those little accidents.

For instance.

One morning when Mr Bump went outside his house he noticed that the chimney pot had come loose in a storm the night before.

"I must fix that before it falls off," thought Mr Bump to himself, and he hurried to his garden shed to fetch a ladder.

It was a very long ladder!

Mr Bump walked up the garden path with the ladder on his shoulder. He turned the corner of the garden path.

CRASH! went the living room window.

"Oh dear," thought Mr Bump, and he turned to see what had happened.

CRASH! went the kitchen window behind him.

"Oh dear," thought Mr Bump again, and he rested the ladder against the wall of the house so that he could climb up on to the roof to mend the chimney pot.

CRASH! went the bedroom window!

So you can see how Mr Bump had his little accidents!

Mr Bump had had many jobs, but somehow they never seemed to last very long.

As soon as anything got lost or broken or splintered or chipped or snapped or cracked or torn or burst or wrenched or crunched or split or slit, Mr Bump got the blame.

For instance.

When Mr Bump worked on a farm, he tripped over the farm dog and spilt the milk which he was carrying for the farmer's wife, and which the farm cat lapped up.

For instance.

When Mr Bump was a postman, he got his hand stuck in a pillar-box, and they had to fetch the fire brigade to come and set him free.

For instance.

When Mr Bump was a bus conductor, he fell off the bus and couldn't catch it up again, and all the passengers travelled without having to pay.

For instance.

When Mr Bump was a carpenter, he found that when he was hammering nails he hammered his thumb most of the time and the nail hardly at all.

In order to recover from this series of rather unfortunate happenings, Mr Bump decided to take a holiday. There he could think about what sort of job he could do where he wouldn't be such a nuisance to everybody.

So off he set to the station to catch a train to the seaside.

While Mr Bump was on holiday, several things happened.

For instance.

He fell off a boat into the sea and the lifeboat had to come and rescue him.

For instance.

One day when he was quietly walking along the beach minding his own business he got his foot stuck in a bucket, and as he couldn't get it off he had to walk round with it on his foot for hours.

For instance.

Another time he was walking along the beach, he walked straight into a large hole that somebody had dug, and he had to stay there all night because he couldn't climb out on his own.

However, despite all these little accidents Mr Bump enjoyed his holiday, and while he was there he had a splendid idea about what sort of job he should do.

It was quite the best idea Mr Bump had ever had. An absolutely splendid idea.

And now Mr Bump works happily for Mr Barley the farmer.

Mr Barley has a rather large apple orchard on his farm, and that's where Mr Bump works.

Mr Bump's job is picking apples. But he doesn't use a ladder to climb up the tree to pick the apples like other apple pickers.

Oh no. Mr Bump has a much better way of picking apples than that!

He just walks about!

And before long Mr Bump being Mr Bump walks into a tree.

BUMP!

And down falls an apple. And Mr Bump catches it.

This makes the job of apple picking much easier, and Mr Bump is very pleased about his new job, and Mr Barley is very pleased about his new apple picker.

So you see the story of Mr Bump isn't such a sad story after all. And if you ever bump yourself you know what to do, don't you?

Go and eat an apple picked by Mr Bump, and then you won't feel your bump at all.

You'll remember that the next time you have a bump, won't you?

Good!

3 Great Offers for MR.MEN Fans!

MR. MEN TOKEN

1 New Mr. Men or Little Miss Library Bus Presentation Cases

A brand new stronger, roomier school bus library box, with sturdy carrying handle and stay-closed fasteners.
The full colour, wipe-clean boxes make a great home for your full collection.
They're just £5.99 inc P&P and free bookmark!

☐ MR. MEN   ☐ LITTLE MISS (please tick and order overleaf)

PLEASE STICK YOUR 50P COIN HERE

2 Door Hangers and Posters

In every Mr. Men and Little Miss book like this one, you will find a special token. Collect 6 tokens and we will send you a brilliant Mr. Men or Little Miss poster and a Mr. Men or Little Miss double sided full colour bedroom door hanger of your choice. Simply tick your choice in the list and tape a 50p coin for your two items to this page.

Door Hangers (please tick)
☐ Mr. Nosey & Mr. Muddle
☐ Mr. Slow & Mr. Busy
☐ Mr. Messy & Mr. Quiet
☐ Mr. Perfect & Mr. Forgetful
☐ Little Miss Fun & Little Miss Late
☐ Little Miss Helpful & Little Miss Tidy
☐ Little Miss Busy & Little Miss Brainy
☐ Little Miss Star & Little Miss Fun

Posters (please tick)
☐ MR.MEN
☐ LITTLE MISS

3 Sixteen Beautiful Fridge Magnets – any **2** for **£2.00!** inc.P&P

They're very special collector's items!
Simply tick your first and second* choices from the list below
of any 2 characters!

1st Choice
- [ ] Mr. Happy
- [ ] Mr. Lazy
- [ ] Mr. Topsy-Turvy
- [ ] Mr. Bounce
- [ ] Mr. Bump
- [ ] Mr. Small
- [ ] Mr. Snow
- [ ] Mr. Wrong

- [ ] Mr. Daydream
- [ ] Mr. Tickle
- [ ] Mr. Greedy
- [ ] Mr. Funny
- [ ] Little Miss Giggles
- [ ] Little Miss Splendid
- [ ] Little Miss Naughty
- [ ] Little Miss Sunshine

2nd Choice
- [ ] Mr. Happy
- [ ] Mr. Lazy
- [ ] Mr. Topsy-Turvy
- [ ] Mr. Bounce
- [ ] Mr. Bump
- [ ] Mr. Small
- [ ] Mr. Snow
- [ ] Mr. Wrong

- [ ] Mr. Daydream
- [ ] Mr. Tickle
- [ ] Mr. Greedy
- [ ] Mr. Funny
- [ ] Little Miss Giggles
- [ ] Little Miss Splendid
- [ ] Little Miss Naughty
- [ ] Little Miss Sunshine

*Only in case your first choice is out of stock.

---- TO BE COMPLETED BY AN ADULT ----

**To apply for any of these great offers, ask an adult to complete the coupon below and send it with
the appropriate payment and tokens, if needed, to MR. MEN OFFERS, PO BOX 7, MANCHESTER M19 2HD**

- [ ] Please send ____ Mr. Men Library case(s) and/or ____ Little Miss Library case(s) at £5.99 each inc P&P
- [ ] Please send a poster and door hanger as selected overleaf. I enclose six tokens plus a 50p coin for P&P
- [ ] Please send me ____ pair(s) of Mr. Men/Little Miss fridge magnets, as selected above at £2.00 inc P&P

Fan's Name _____

Address _____

_____ **Postcode** _____

Date of Birth _____

Name of Parent/Guardian _____

Total amount enclosed £ _____

- [ ] **I enclose a cheque/postal order payable to Egmont Books Limited**
- [ ] **Please charge my MasterCard/Visa/Amex/Switch or Delta account** (delete as appropriate)

Card Number

Expiry date ____/____   **Signature** _____

Please allow 28 days for delivery. We reserve the right to change the terms of this offer at any time but we offer
a 14 day money back guarantee. This does not affect your statutory rights. Data Protection Act: If you do not wish
to receive other similar offers from us or companies we recommend, please tick this box [ ]. Offers apply to UK only.

MR.MEN   LITTLE MISS
Mr. Men and Little Miss™ & ©Mrs. Roger Hargreaves

CUT ALONG DOTTED LINE AND RETURN THIS WHOLE PAGE